BOOK ONE

DISNEY PRESS
New York • Los Angeles

Andy was a young boy with a *big* imagination. He loved playing with his toys. His favorite was Sheriff Woody, a pull-string cowboy. But there was something Andy didn't know. When no one was around, his toys came to life!

One day Woody called a meeting. Andy's family was moving soon. He wanted to make sure all the toys were ready. But Woody had other news, too.

"Andy's birthday party has been moved to today," he said.

The toys were worried. A birthday party meant new toys. What if Andy liked his new toys more than he liked the ones he already had?

Woody sent the Green Army Men downstairs to report on Andy's presents. As he opened the last one, the radio cut out.

Andy had gotten a new toy named Buzz Lightyear. Buzz did not know he was a toy. He thought he was a real space ranger!

Buzz was a hit with the other toys. But the real surprise came at bedtime. When Andy got into bed, he took Buzz with him instead of Woody!

LIGHTYEAR

One evening, Andy's mom suggested a trip to Pizza Planet. She told Andy he could bring one toy. Woody wanted to be picked. He tried to knock Buzz behind a desk, but instead the space ranger fell out the window.

"It was an accident!" said Woody. But the other toys didn't believe him.

Suddenly, Andy burst into the room. When he couldn't find Buzz, he decided to take Woody with him instead.

As Woody and Andy got into the car, a figure emerged from the bushes. It was Buzz! He leaped onto the car's bumper. He was on his way to Pizza Planet.

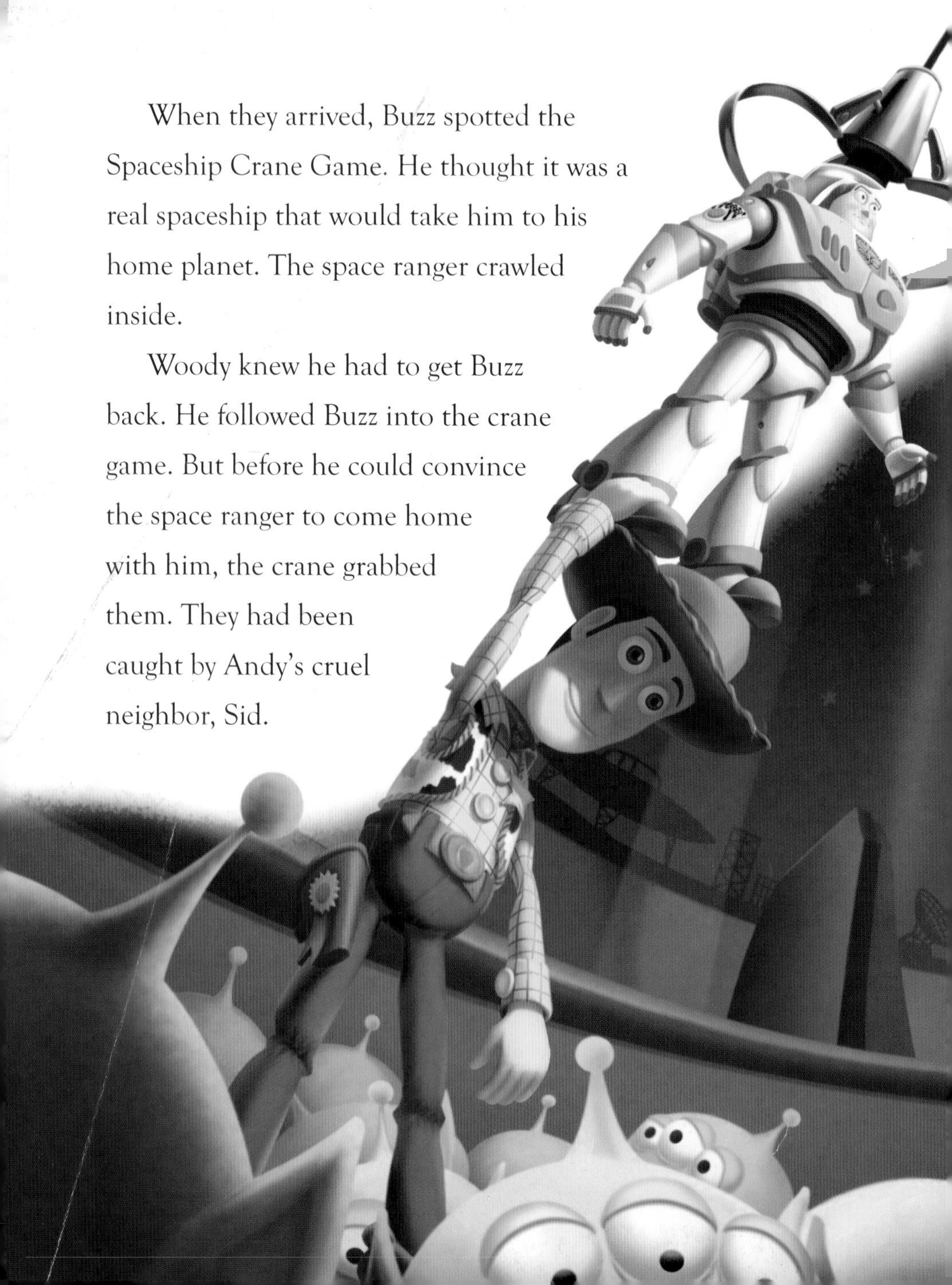

When they arrived, Buzz spotted the Spaceship Crane Game. He thought it was a real spaceship that would take him to his home planet. The space ranger crawled inside.

Woody knew he had to get Buzz back. He followed Buzz into the crane game. But before he could convince the space ranger to come home with him, the crane grabbed them. They had been caught by Andy's cruel neighbor, Sid.

Sid brought the toys home and carried them to his bedroom. The room was dark and eerie. Strange mutant toys that Sid had created by mixing parts of other toys hid everywhere. Terrified, Buzz and Woody ran into the hall—and straight into Sid's dog, Scud.

The toys fled and became separated from each other.

Buzz ducked through an open door. Inside, he heard a voice say, “Calling Buzz Lightyear. This is Star Command.”

An ad for the Buzz Lightyear toy was on TV. Buzz was shocked.

“Is it true?” he whispered. “Am I really . . . a toy?”

Desperate to prove that he was a real space ranger, Buzz tried to fly. But he crashed to the floor, breaking off his arm.

“Look at me!” Buzz moaned when Woody found him. “I can’t even fly out the window.”

The window! That gave Woody an idea. Looking out Sid’s window, he called to his friends in Andy’s room.

But when the toys saw Woody holding Buzz's arm, they grew angry. They thought he had hurt Buzz.

Woody sadly turned away from the window. He and Buzz were stuck. How would they ever get home?

Just then, the mutant toys grabbed Buzz's broken arm. Woody thought they were trying to hurt the space ranger. But instead they fixed him.

As they finished, Sid burst into the room. He grabbed Buzz and tied a rocket to his back. He planned to set it off first thing in the morning!

Buzz was too sad to care about the rocket. “You were right,” he told Woody. “I’m not a space ranger. I’m just a toy.”

Woody tried to cheer him up. “Over in that house is a kid who thinks you are the greatest. And it’s not because you’re a space ranger. It’s because you’re a toy. You are *his* toy.”

Finally, Buzz realized Woody was right. Being a toy *was* important. They had to find a way back to Andy.

Woody gathered the mutant toys. He was going to need their help.

"We'll have to break a few rules," Woody told them. "But if it works, it'll help everyone."

The mutants agreed and went to take their places.

The next morning, as Sid prepared to light Buzz's rocket, the mutant toys crept toward him. One by one they surrounded the boy. Terrified, he ran off, promising never to hurt another toy.

The mutants cheered. But Buzz and Woody had to get going. Andy's family moving van was leaving. If they didn't catch up, they'd be left behind in another neighborhood.

The two friends rushed after the van. Barking, Scud raced behind them. Buzz managed to climb onto the van's bumper, but the cruel dog caught Woody.

Buzz bravely leaped off the bumper and fought off the dog. Woody pulled himself onto the van. But there was a problem. Now Buzz was stranded on the road!

Woody scrambled into the van and found the box that contained Andy's toys. Using RC Car's remote control, he sent the car back to pick up Buzz.

The toys thought Woody was trying to get rid of RC, too. Shouting angrily, they threw him out of the van.

Woody and Buzz climbed aboard RC and took off. But his batteries did not last long.

Suddenly, Buzz remembered something. “Woody! The rocket!” he yelled.

Woody lit the fuse. They soared into the sky.

Buzz dropped RC into the van. Then he extended his wings, freeing them from the rocket. Seconds later, they dropped gently through the sunroof of Andy’s car. Woody and Buzz were back where they belonged.